MY NINJA HAVE BEEN DEFENDING THE WORLD OF NINJAGO FOR TEN YEARS. THIS ANNIVERSARY IS A CHANCE TO CELEBRATE AND REMEMBER OUR BEST ADVENTURES. READY? LET'S BEGIN . . .

. . . RIGHT AFTER YOU ASSEMBLE THE LLOYD MINIFIGURE IN A CELEBRATORY OUTFIT.

HOW TO BUILD LLOYD

THE FIRST NINJA MISSION WAS SUPER HARD! SEE FOR YOURSELF—GO THROUGH THE MAZE AND NUMBER THE GOLDEN WEAPONS IN THE ORDER YOU COLLECT THEM.

ON A SCALE OF ONE TO TEN, I RATE THE DIFFICULTY OF THIS MISSION AT . . . ONE MILLION!

START

FINISH

Answers on page 31.

ONCE, ONE OF THE NINJA FELL INTO THE HANDS OF GARMADON AND HIS SKELETON GANG. FIND THE MATCHING SYMBOLS—THEY WILL REVEAL WHO WAS KIDNAPPED.

KNOCKING AROUND A FEW BONES BROUGHT THE NINJA TEAM TOGETHER. COMPLETE THE SKELETON SEQUENCE BY WRITING THE NUMBERS OF THE CORRECT POSES.

1
2
3
4
5

Answers on page 31.

WITH THE HELP OF MASTER WU, THE NINJA REACHED THEIR TRUE POTENTIAL. SEE HOW HARD THEY TRAINED AND THEN MATCH THEIR SHADOWS.

1

PRACTICE MAKES PERFECT!

2

3

4

5

I'D RATHER TRAIN FOR A NOODLE-EATING CONTEST...

5

Answers on page 31.

SSSENSATIONAL! LLOYD WAS ONCE FRIENDS WITH A SERPENTINE LEADER. USE THE HINTS TO FIND THE RIGHT GENERAL.

THE GENERAL:
- **HAS ONLY ONE HEAD**
- **DOESN'T HAVE HORNS**
- **IS BEHIND A STAFF**

WOW! LLOYD SUDDENLY BECAME THE GOLDEN NINJA AND AN IDOL FOR MANY. FIND OUT WHY BY SELECTING THE RIGHT FLASH-SHAPED PICTURE PIECE.

THE GOLDEN NINJA IS RUINING THE PHOTOS!

5

GOLDEN GLOW

THE GOLDEN MECH USED BY LLOYD TO FIGHT THE OVERLORD'S STONE ARMY SUFFERED DURING THE LAST CLASH.

YOU LOOK BAD, AND YOU'VE LOST YOUR SHINE. I'M GONNA FIX YOU RIGHT UP!

A MONTH LATER

ARMS WORK. LEGS ARE FINE TOO. A BIT OF POLISHING, AND YOU'LL BE GOOD AS NEW!

A WEEK LATER

LLOYD! WANNA PLAY A NEW VIDEO GAME?

I CAN'T. I HAVE TO POLISH THE MECH.

ANOTHER WEEK LATER

LLOYD! WANNA GO TO THE MOVIES?

SORRY, GUYS! I HAVE TO POLISH THE MECH.

A FEW DAYS LATER

LLOYD! WE GOTTA GO FIGHT THE STONE WARRIORS!

GIVE ME A SEC! I NEED TO FINISH POLISHING THE MECH!

WHAT A WASTE! THE MECH IS GONNA GET DUSTY NOW ANYWAY.

AND THE STONE ARMY WILL SEE ITS GLOW FROM MILES AWAY!

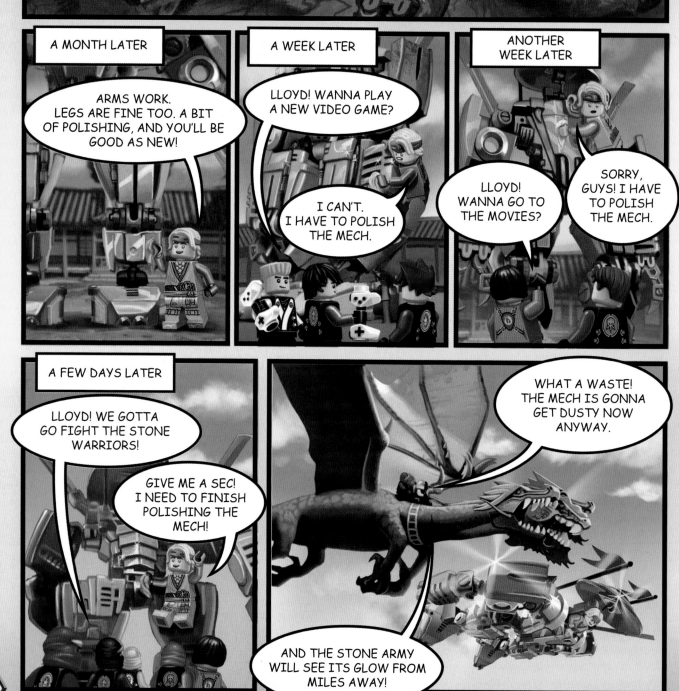

THIS IS WHAT ZANE LOOKS LIKE WHEN HE REMEMBERS THE DAY HE MET PIXAL. CONNECT THE DOTS AND BRING BACK THE MEMORY.

WOW! WU FOUGHT FOR EVIL, AND GARMADON FOR GOOD. RECREATE THE DUEL. ENTER G AND W IN THE BLANK SQUARES TO MAKE THE OPPONENTS APPEAR TWICE IN EACH ROW.

Answers on page 31.

TIME TO RECALL ZANE'S MEETING WITH THE CRYPTOR GANG. LEAD HIM THROUGH THE MAZE SO THAT HE MEETS ALL THE NINDROIDS ON HIS WAY, WITHOUT TAKING THE SAME PATH TWICE.

START

FINISH

HEY, *WE* WERE SUPPOSED TO SCRAP *HIM*, NOT THE OTHER WAY ROUND!

9

Answer on page 31.

THE TOURNAMENT HOST, MASTER CHEN, FORCED THE LOSERS TO WORK AT HIS NOODLE FACTORY. UNTANGLE THE NOODLES TO SEE WHO WAS HAPPY WITH THE PUNISHMENT.

CHECK OUT THE LOOK ON CHEN'S FACE WHEN KAI DESTROYED HIS WEAPON! ENTER THE CORRECT PARTS IN THEIR SPACES TO SEE HOW THE STAFF OF ELEMENTS WAS BUILT.

MORRO IS AN EVIL SPIRIT WHO ONCE POSSESSED A NINJA. FIND OUT WHO IT WAS BY CHOOSING THE CHARACTER WHO SHOULD APPEAR WHERE THE QUESTION MARK IS.

COLE WAS A GHOST FOR A WHILE TOO. RECALL THOSE SPOOKY TIMES AND COLOR THE NINJA TO MAKE HIM TRANSPARENT.

ONE GOOD THING ABOUT BEING A GHOST WAS THAT I DIDN'T HAVE TO COME UP WITH A HALLOWEEN COSTUME.

Answer on page 31.

AT THE MERE MENTION OF MEETING THE PIRATES, THE NINJA GET SEASICK. LOOK CLOSELY AND CIRCLE THE MISSING PIRATES IN EACH PICTURE.

Answers on page 31.

ONCE THE NINJA WERE IMPRISONED BY NADAKHAN, THE PIRATE CAPTAIN. DON'T BELIEVE IT? DRAW LINES TO CONNECT THE SCATTERED PICTURE PIECES.

NYA'S FAVORITE PART OF HER WEDDING TO NADAKHAN? BREAKING UP THE CEREMONY! RECREATE THE EVENT BY CONNECTING ALL THE ELEMENTS OF THE PATH IN THE GRID.

START

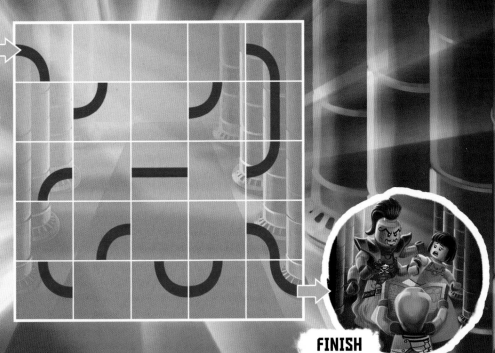

FINISH

THE NINJA HAVE NEVER BEEN AS TIRED AS THEY WERE WHEN THEY CLEANED THE MUSEUM! MATCH THE SCULPTURES COVERED DURING CLEANING TO THE CORRECT VILLAINS.

GOOD THING THE TIME BLADES ARE NOTHING BUT A MEMORY. FIGURE OUT THE COLOR OF EACH BLADE AND ADD THE COLOR NEXT TO THE RIGHT HINT.

1
THE FORWARD TIME BLADE IS GREEN.

2
THE SLOW-MO TIME BLADE IS THE ONLY ONE POINTING SIDEWAYS.

3
THE PAUSE TIME BLADE IS BETWEEN THE ORANGE AND GREEN BLADE.

4
THE REVERSAL TIME BLADE AND THE PAUSE TIME BLADE ARE HELD BY THE SAME PERSON.

Answers on page 32.

HERE'S A MEMORY WORTH ERASING! FIND AND CIRCLE THE PATH TO UNDO THE TIME PUNCH, A POWERFUL AGING BLOW.

FINISH

START

A

B

C

D

E

WHEN THE EFFECTS OF THE TIME PUNCH WORE OFF, I FELT AS IF I WERE ONLY A HUNDRED YEARS OLD AGAIN!

Answer on page 32.

HA! THE SONS OF GARMADON, THE GANG THAT HAS ROAMED NINJAGO CITY, ARE NOW BEHIND BARS. LOOK INSIDE THE PRISON CELL AND DRAW LINES TO CONNECT THE FRAGMENTS WITH THE CORRECT VILLAINS.

THE ONI MASKS WERE ONCE VERY POWERFUL, AND EVEN BROUGHT BACK THE GARMADON! ALTHOUGH THESE WERE THE OLD DAYS, SCRIBBLE OVER THE PLACES WHERE THE THREE DIFFERENT MASKS APPEAR NEXT TO EACH OTHER, JUST IN CASE.

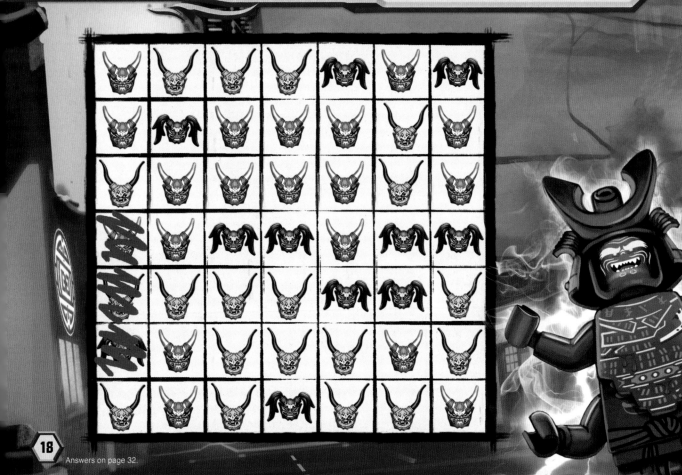

Answers on page 32.

IT WAS SO FUN DEFEATING THE DRAGON HUNTERS! DEFEAT THEM AGAIN BY NUMBERING THE PICTURES FROM THE ONE WITH THE LEAST HUNTERS TO THE ONE WITH THE MOST HUNTERS.

Answers on page 32.

WHEN DEMONS THREATENED THE WORLD OF NINJAGO, THE NINJA TURNED TO ONE OF THEIR ENEMIES FOR HELP. WHO WAS IT? THE COLOR KEY BELOW WILL LEAD YOU TO THE RIGHT CELL.

INVITING A VILLAIN TO THE TEAM? WHAT'S THE WORLD COME TO?

Answer on page 32.

FINALLY IN THE LAND OF NINJAGO, THERE WAS PEACE—AND UNBELIEVABLE BOREDOM. HELP SOLVE THE MOST IMPORTANT MISSION AT THE TIME AND COUNT THE CATS TO REMOVE THEM FROM THE TREE.

THIS WAS NO SIMPLE TASK.

SOON A NEW ENEMY APPEARED IN THE PATH OF THE NINJA: ASPHEERA! CIRCLE THE ARROWS THAT INDICATE WHERE TO MOVE EACH PUZZLE PIECE.

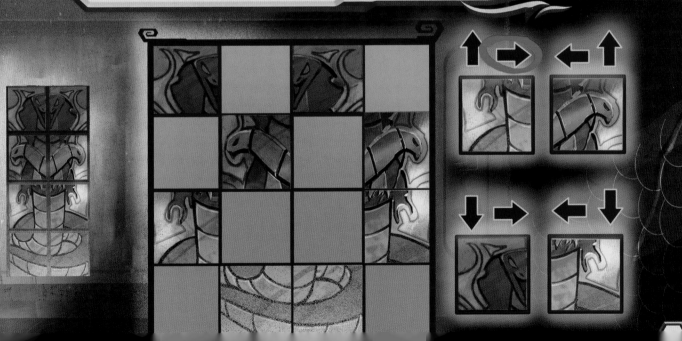

THE GOLDEN STAR OF THE PARTY
BY MARTA LEŚNIAK

Inside the Monastery of Spinjitzu, the ninja convened at the request of Master Wu.

"Ten years have passed since you began standing guard over the land of Ninjago," Master Wu said. "Let us mark this important occasion with a . . . party."

The ninja leaped from their seats, "Great idea!" . . . "Hooray, a party!" . . . "But no clowns! Clowns are dangerous," they called out to one another.

"Remember," Master Wu warned, "only self-control and hard work can protect the planning committee . . . from hiring a clown."

Once the ninja chose a menu and a theme—the color gold—discussing the guest list was all that remained.

"I think we should invite the evildoers we've been fighting for the past ten years, too," Nya said. "After all, without our enemies, our anniversary wouldn't exist."

"Skeletons, Serpentine, Stone Warriors," counted out Cole. "They can come. But an invitation to the *leaders* of those bands is a bad idea."

"Yes. I calculate the risk is too high," Zane agreed.

The day of the anniversary party arrived. Master Wu and his students, all in funky gold costumes, greeted their guests.

"I wasn't expecting to have stage fright," sighed Master Wu, who had prepared a tea-making demonstration for the evening.

"I feel you, Master," admitted Jay, nervous about his stand-up routine.

Soon all the tables were filled with families, friends, and enemies of the ninja. Forgetting past disputes, everyone was swept away by the party atmosphere. "You look great!" . . . "How long's it been?!" . . . "A toast to the ninja!" could be heard.

After dinner, Jay started his show. The blue ninja quickly forgot about stage fright as the audience burst into laughter after each joke. The stiff Stone Warriors even swayed to the rhythm of the hit songs Cole sang.

Master Wu's performance was next.

"First, I will show you my teacup collection. I've described each of them in this catalogue," announced the Master, opening a very thick book.

"YAAAAAAAAWWWNNN!" A bored guest lost interest during page two of the catalogue. A few guests even drifted to sleep. They did not sleep long, however, because they were awoken by loud thunder! Someone shouted, "Supervillains!" and on the horizon Garmadon, Pythor, Samukai, and General Kozu appeared.

The party patrons were terrified. The Serpentines hissed nervously, the Skeletons got goose bumps—despite not having any skin—and the Stone Army turned as pale as limestone.

"Get ready for a riot," moaned Lloyd as the ninja formed a line, ready to defend their guests.

"Is it nice having a secret party?!" Garmadon boomed. "Good thing I found the invitation for those bony blockheads," he added, pointing at the frightened Skeletons. "I asked all around, and you know what I discovered? Not a single one of my buddies got an invitation. So I decided to correct the oversight and invited us myself."

Garmadon reached under his cloak. The rest of the villains did the same. The crowd froze, and the ninja took on even stronger fighting poses. But instead of terrible weapons, in the hands of the evil ones appeared . . . golden hats, wigs, and silly glasses.

Dressed in gold party gear, Garmadon stood on the dance floor and decreed, "Ninja, we will fight you another time. We have come here tonight only as LORDS OF THE DANCE FLOOR! Hit the music!"

The guests, just a little nervous at first, couldn't resist the party vibe. The ninja soon joined in as well.

"Garmadon saved the party," Cole said, sneaking into the conga line that was snaking around the dance floor. "Thanks to him, no one has to watch Master Wu's show!"

THIS IS WHAT JAY LOOKED LIKE BEFORE HE ENTERED A VIDEO GAME THAT TRAPPED PEOPLE! COLOR IN THE NUMBER 1 SQUARES WITH BLUE TO SEE WHAT LEVEL JAY HAS REACHED.

0	0	0	0	0	0	0	0	0
0	0	1	1	0	1	1	1	0
0	0	0	1	0	0	0	1	0
0	0	0	1	0	0	0	1	0
0	0	0	1	0	1	1	1	0
0	0	0	1	0	0	0	1	0
0	0	0	1	0	1	1	1	0
0	0	0	0	0	0	0	0	0

BOOYAH!

IN THE GAME OF PRIME EMPIRE, THERE WAS A LOT OF JUMPING. PRESERVE THE MEMORY—JUMP OVER THE LEVELS BY CONNECTING THE SAME SYMBOLS ON ADJACENT BOARDS.

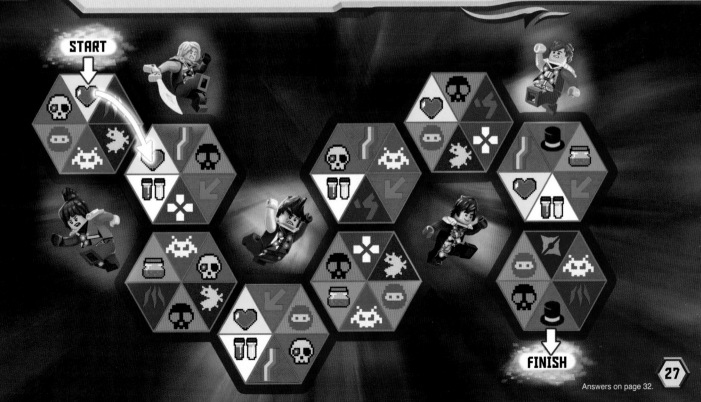

START

FINISH

Answers on page 32.

KAI AND NYA WERE ONCE STUCK WITH THE QUARRELING TRIBES OF GECKLES AND MUNCE. SEE HOW EACH OF THEM REMEMBERED THE TRIBES AND MARK TEN DIFFERENCES BETWEEN THE PICTURES BELOW.

Answers on page 32.

THE NINJA MET A FEW VILLAINS WHO PRETENDED TO BE SOMEONE ELSE ENTIRELY. OUTLINE THE PORTRAIT SETS ON THE LEFT IN THE GRID. THE REMAINING PORTRAIT SHOWS THE VILLAIN IN DISGUISE.

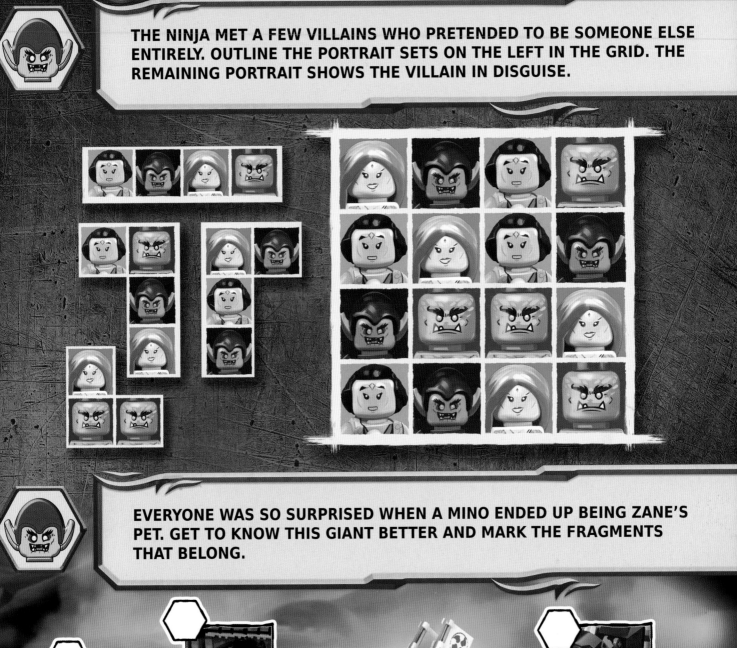

EVERYONE WAS SO SURPRISED WHEN A MINO ENDED UP BEING ZANE'S PET. GET TO KNOW THIS GIANT BETTER AND MARK THE FRAGMENTS THAT BELONG.

Answers on page 32.

IT'S BEEN AN AMAZING TEN YEARS, BUT IT'S TIME TO SET OUT ON A NEW ADVENTURE. FIND THE ITEMS THE NINJA HAVE ALREADY PACKED AND CHECK THEM OFF THE LIST!

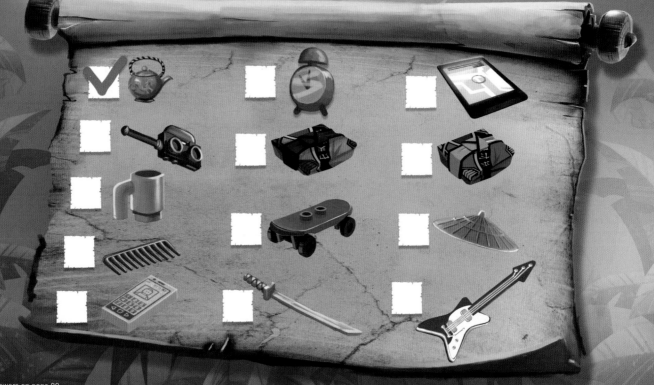

Answers on page 32.

ANSWERS

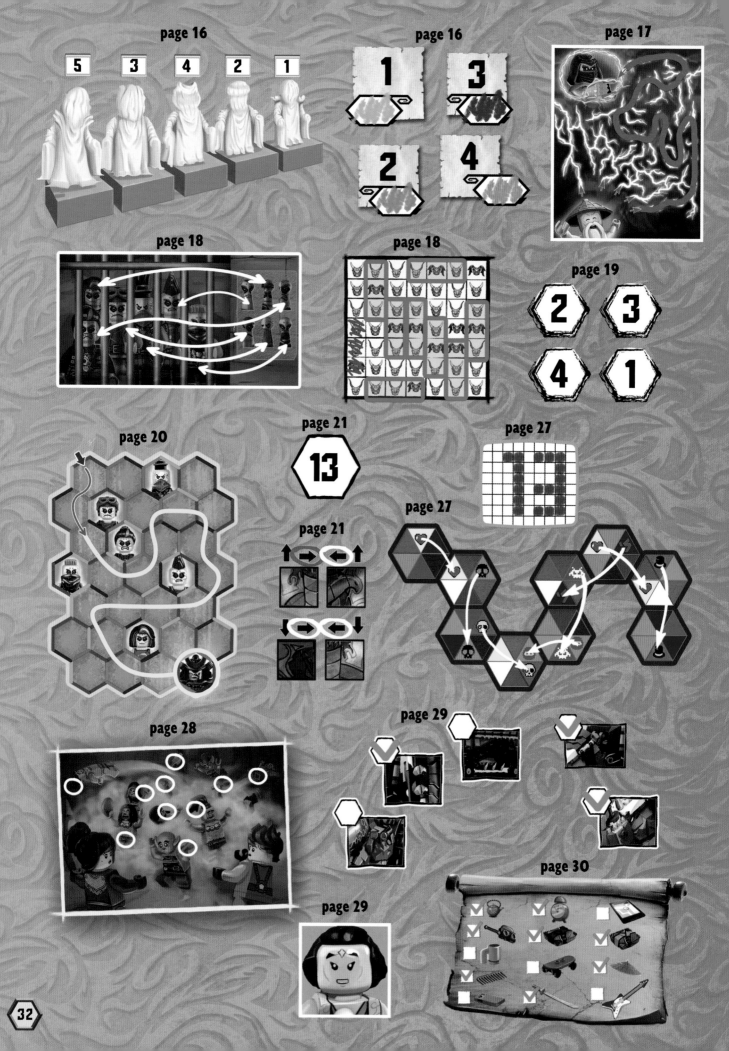

page 16

page 16

page 17

page 18

page 18

page 19

page 20

page 21

page 27

page 21

page 27

page 28

page 29

page 30

page 29